Forest Queen

Comma

Great Egg Fly

Egg Fly

Tawny Coster

Polyphemus Moth

Japanese Emperor

Tailed Emperor

Monarch

Large Tree Nymph

Cairns Birdwing

Guatemalan Cracker

To Lena, who, in my eyes, always has a butterfly on her finger.
And to those most gracious Gratch girls, especially Barbara,
Laura, and Mina, for their constant inspiration. —A.M.

To Karen Carlson, Queen of Metamorphosis.
And special thanks to Winston Barton. —K.H.

All rights reserved.

Published in the United States by Schwartz & Wade Books,

an imprint of Random House Children's Books,

a division of Random House, Inc., New York.

Schwartz & Wade Books and colophon

are trademarks of Random House, Inc.

www.randomhouse.com/kids

Educators and librarians,

for a variety of teaching tools,

visit us at www.randomhouse.com/teachers

Library of Congress Cataloging-

in-Publication Data

Madison, Alan. Velma Gratch and

the way cool butterfly / Alan Madison ;

illustrated by Kevin Hawkes.

—1st ed. p. cm.

First Edition

Summary:

Velma starts first grade in the shadow of her memorable

older sisters, and while her newfound interest in

butterflies helps her to stand out, it also leads to

an interesting complication.

ISBN 978-0-375-83597-1 (trade)

ISBN 978-0-375-93597-8 (lib. bdg.)

[1. Butterflies—Fiction.

2. Schools—Fiction.

3. Individuality—Fiction.

4. Sisters—Fiction.]

I. Hawkes, Kevin, ill. II. Title.

PZ7.M2587Vel 2007 [E]—dc22

2006030978

PRINTED IN CHINA

10 9 8 7 6 5 4 3 2 1

velma
gratch
&
the
way
cool
butterfly

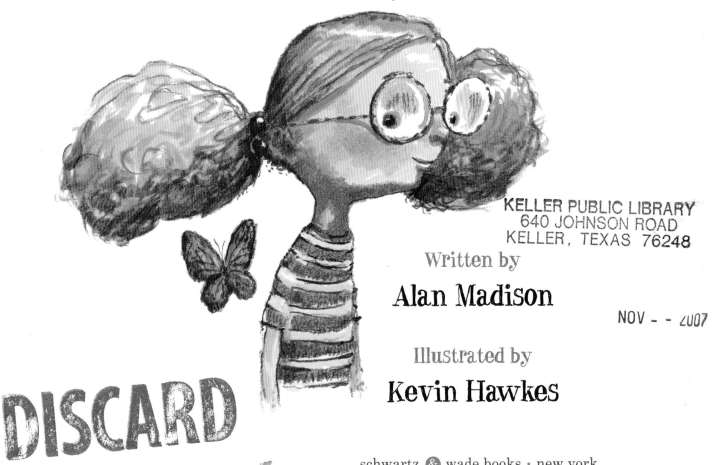

Written by

Alan Madison

Illustrated by

Kevin Hawkes

schwartz & wade books · new york

Velma Gratch was the youngest of the three Gratch sisters. Frieda, the oldest, had gone through first grade first, followed by Fiona. Now it was Velma's turn.

The chorus teacher remembered
Frieda best because she had a voice
like an angel.

The gym teacher remembered
Fiona best because she ran like
the devil.

And the first-grade teacher,
Mr. Plexipuss, fondly remembered
both sisters because of Frieda's
miraculous math and Fiona's
spectacular spelling.

Everyone from the class guinea pig to the principal had magnificent
memories of the older Gratch girls. But they could hardly even recall
Velma's name.

This made Velma feel as if she did not belong in the first grade at all.
She wanted to curl into a ball and roll right back into kindergarten.

"Of course you belong," cooed Velma's mother, trying to cheer her
up. "You've only just begun. Soon everybody will notice you."

Velma couldn't wait. She needed to be noticed—now!

In chorus she sang loudest so that the teacher could hear her best.

In gym she ran slowest so that the teacher could see her best.

And in class she refused to read and muddled her math.

Mr. Plexipuss lamented that she was the first Gratch sister ever sent to the principal's office. This brought a small smile to Velma's lips.

"Littlest Gratch, why are you singing so loudly in chorus and running so slowly in gym?" inquired Principal Crossly.

"Because," answered Velma, "I want you to remember me just like you remember Frieda and Fiona."

The principal's owlish eyes opened wide. "But my dear, those Gratches are remembered for *good* things."

Velma's small smile pretzel-twisted into a full-blown frown.

Science was Velma's favorite subject. She had learned many fabulous facts, like how a rainbow is born and why a volcano burps. The latest lesson was about butterflies.

Mr. Plexipuss explained that a butterfly starts as an egg. The egg turns into a caterpillar. The caterpillar disappears into a chrysalis, which is a little sack, and does not come out until it has changed into a beautiful butterfly.

He called this changing *metamorphosis*. Velma didn't want to forget this extra-long word, so she repeated it again and again as she walked home.

"Metamorphosis. Metamorphosis. Metamorphosis."

"Frieda, when you were in first grade, did you study butterflies?"
Velma asked her oldest sister.

"No, we learned worms," Frieda replied.

"Fiona, when you were in first grade, did you study butterflies?"
Velma asked her middle sister.

"No, we found out about frogs," Fiona stated.

"Well," said Velma proudly, "we are studying butterflies and . . .
and . . . metal-more-for-this."

"That's way cool," Frieda declared, and Fiona bobbled her head
in "way cool" agreement.

Velma read everything in the library about butterflies. She discovered that there are 20,000 different kinds—which was a lot. She adored the ones with colorful names: brown elfin, frosted flasher, sleepy orange. And the ones with funny names: comma, question mark, American snout. Not to mention the ones with strange names: morpho, painted lady, gossamer-wing.

But her favorite butterfly of all was the orange and black monarch. When it got cold, all the monarchs would fly south to Mexico to stay warm. Velma thought this was an amazing coincidence, because last winter vacation she and her family had also flown south to Mexico to stay warm.

In science, Mr. Plexipuss announced that they would take a class trip to the Butterfly Conservatory, a place where real butterflies were collected and cared for. Because Velma didn't want to forget this extra-long word, she repeated it again and again as she walked home.

"Conservatory. Conservatory. Conservatory. Conservatory."

"Frieda, did you take a class trip in first grade?" Velma asked her oldest sister.

"Absolutely. We went to the museum," Frieda replied.

"Fiona, did you take a class trip in first grade?" Velma asked her middle sister.

"Absolutely. We went to the aquarium," Fiona stated.

"Well," said Velma proudly, "we're going to the can . . . can . . . can-serve-the-story."

"That's way cool," Frieda declared, and Fiona bobbled her head in "way cool" agreement.

The Butterfly Conservatory was surrounded by fancy flower beds and bedecked with banners of butterflies. Velma was so excited, her knobby knees wobbled, her spaghetti arms trembled, and her carroty curls shook.

A sharp-nosed woman holding a clipboard introduced herself. "I am your tour guide. Inside, a butterfly might land on you. But please don't touch its wings. Does anyone know why?"

Velma's hand shot up. "Because they're made of teeny tiny scales that could rub off like dust, and that is not good," she explained.

"Precisely," said the guide. "What's your name?"

"I'm Velma, the youngest of the three Gratch sisters."

"Hmmm, I don't think I know your sisters," the guide commented as they entered the rain-forested room.

It was a magical space slathered in tall trees and tangled vines. Water gurgled over rocks, and butterflies of every variety—giant swallowtails, short-tailed skippers, pygmy blues, and best of all, monarchs—flew up to forever.

The guide explained that when it got colder in a couple of weeks, she would take the monarchs into the park and let them go free, so that they could fly to Mexico. This traveling was called *migration*.

Because Velma didn't want to forget this extra-long word, she repeated it again and again as she walked through the rain forest. "Migration. Migration. Migration."

A gorgeous green comma rested on Randy's head. The class oohed.

A baby brown elfin settled on Sandy's nose. The class aahed.

A big blue morpho alighted on Andy's shoulder. The class gasped. But not one single butterfly landed on any part of Velma.

"Time to leave," instructed Mr. Plexipuss as they neared the exit.

A tear formed in a distant corner of Velma's eye. All she wanted was one single tingly touch of a butterfly.

On a nearby branch sat a most lovely monarch. How she yearned to pet those velvety wings! She moved slowly. The class was leaving. One more inch . . . It was so pretty. She froze. If she touched its wings, it might . . .

Velma couldn't do it. She couldn't hurt a butterfly.

"Come now, Velma, we have to go."

Sadly Velma turned away. And at that very moment the most marvelous thing happened.

The monarch hopped from its branch and roosted
right on Velma's finger!

Delicate wings slowly folding,
antennae twitching,
weightless and wondrous,
the insect sat.

Velma was in heaven.

"The bus is waiting," her teacher called.

Velma placed her finger next to the branch. "Bye-bye, butterfly," she whispered. But the monarch didn't move.

"We're closing," said the guide.

Velma lightly blew on the butterfly. It didn't budge.

Without ever touching the butterfly's wings, everyone tried to get the monarch to fly, crawl, or walk off Velma's finger. But nothing worked.

At last Velma was told to leave with the butterfly still perched on her pointer.

It stayed there on the bus ride home.

It stayed there when she slept and was still there when she awoke.

It stayed during gym.

Math.

Reading!

Ballet!!!

Soccer!!!!

Day in and day out, it stayed put on that pointer.

Soon everyone, from the class guinea pig to the
principal, knew about Velma and her butterfly.

Mr. Plexipuss lamented that Velma was positively the first Gratch ever sent to the principal's office twice! This stuck an oversize frown on Velma's face.

"Velma," Principal Crossly commanded, "it is time for the butterfly to go."

"Oh, I've tried to get it to go," Velma moaned, "but it just *won't.*"

"Well, no one will ever forget this," the principal fumed.

Velma's frown pretzel-twisted into a small smile.

"Hey, I know what to do," she proclaimed. "My-gray-sun!"

Velma paraded Principal Crossly, Mr. Plexipuss, her class, Frieda, and Fiona to the park. Car horns honked. People yelled. But despite all the commotion, the monarch did not move.

A cool wind from the west blew through the field. In the middle stood the tour guide from the conservatory, carefully opening an enormous sack. A single monarch butterfly stepped out, looked around, and flitted away. It was trailed by ten, then ten more, soaring up and up until the sky overflowed with thick clouds of orange and black.

"What's happening?" wondered Frieda.

"Why are you letting them go?" demanded Fiona.

"Migration," answered the guide.

"My-gray-sun," repeated Velma.

The wind tousled Velma's hair and tickled her butterfly's wings. The monarch jumped onto her nose, as if to give her a kiss, and then took flight to join its friends. Over the treetops it flew, over the skyscrapers, and up into the wild blue, orange, and black yonder on its way to Mexico.

"Velma!" shouted Principal Crossly, and every eye turned toward her.

Oh, no, fretted Velma, sure that she was about to become the only Gratch ever sent to the principal's office three times.

"That was way cool," the principal said. And one and all bobbled their heads in "way cool" agreement.

Then, with her fine finger where the monarch had sat still atingle, Velma—followed by her two sisters—floated home.

Large Tiger

Meadow Argus

Rajah Brookes Birdwing

Blue-Green Reflector

Large Copper

88

Blue Morpho

Tiger Swallowtail

Large Spotted Acraea